THE
GHOSTLY
GAME

BLOOMSBURY EDUCATION
Bloomsbury Publishing Plc
50 Bedford Square, London, WC1B 3DP, UK

BLOOMSBURY, BLOOMSBURY EDUCATION and the Diana logo
are trademarks of Bloomsbury Publishing Plc

First published in 2011 by A & C Black Limited, an imprint of
Bloomsbury Publishing Plc, as *Is There Anybody There?*

This edition published in Great Britain in 2019 by Bloomsbury Publishing Plc
Text copyright © Maggie Pearson, 2011
Illustrations copyright © Nelson Evergreen, 2011

Maggie Pearson and Nelson Evergreen have asserted their rights under the Copyright,
Designs and Patents Act, 1988, to be identified as Author and Illustrator of this work

A catalogue record for this book is available from the British Library

ISBN: PB: 978-1-4729-6890-6; ePDF: 978-1-4729-6891-3; ePub: 978-1-4729-6888-3

2 4 6 8 10 9 7 5 3 1

Typeset by Integra Software Services Pvt. Ltd.

Printed and bound in China by Leo Paper Products

To find out more about our authors and books visit
www.bloomsbury.com and sign up for our newsletters

recommended by

www.catchup.org

Catch Up is a charity which aims to address the problem of underachievement
that has its roots in literacy and numeracy difficulties.

THE GHOSTLY GAME

MAGGIE PEARSON

Illustrated by NELSON EVERGREEN

BLOOMSBURY EDUCATION

LONDON   OXFORD   NEW YORK   NEW DELHI   SYDNEY

For Tom

CONTENTS

Chapter One

Scared

I'm scared.

I admit it. I'm scared.

Walking home from school in the dark, I hear footsteps behind me. I turn but there's no-one there.

A shadow moves in a doorway. That's all it is. A shadow.

I'm still scared.

The others think it's all over. "He's gone," they say. "Sorted."

I know different.

I've got proof.

Chapter Two

It's Not a Party

It all began last Halloween. Mum was working the evening shift in A and E. I was going to have a quiet night in. Watch TV. Maybe make a start on my history project.

Maybe not.

Mum said, "I don't like leaving you on your own, Scott."

"Why not?" I said. "You've done it before."

"Not on Halloween."

"Halloween is no big deal. I'll be fine."

"Jaz's mum says Jaz hasn't got any plans for this evening," she said. "Why don't you ask her round?"

Jaz and I, we like the same music, the same movies. And I knew Mum would wear me down in the end. So I called her.

Mum went off happy.

I just had time to put on a clean shirt and run a comb through my hair before the doorbell rang. I opened the door.

"Hi, Scott," said Jaz. "I brought Mo with me. Is that OK?"

It was not OK. Mo is like bad news waiting to happen.

"It's not a party, Mo," I told her.

"I can see that," she said, looking past me.

Then Lee turned up. He was zig-zagging his bike from one side of the road to the other. In his hand he had a DVD.

"Got it at last!" he yelled. "'Planet of the Undead'! This one will blow your socks off!" He dropped his bike on the drive and slid past me into the living room.

"Come on in, girls," he said. "You're just in time for the big picture."

We got some drinks and nibbles and sat down to watch.

Half an hour later I hit the 'off' button. Even Lee had stopped laughing by then. I'd sat through some rubbish horror with him in the past but 'Planet of the Undead' was the worst yet.

Jaz had her head in a cushion and Mo was pretending to be asleep.

"So! What do we do now?" said Lee. "Send out for a pizza?"

"There's a pizza in the freezer," I said. "If you really want one."

"Not that much," he said.

"I've got a better idea," said Mo.

"Better than pizza?" said Lee.

Mo didn't answer. She was fishing in her bag. Then she held up a pack of cards.

These weren't playing cards. As Mo began laying them out in a circle on the table, I saw they were marked with all the letters of the alphabet, plus the words YES and NO.

"It's Halloween, right?" said Mo. "The night when ghosts walk and witches ride and all that stuff. So why don't we try and magic up a real, live ghost or two?"

"Ghosts?" I said. "In this house? You'll be lucky!"

"Who believes in ghosts anyway?" said Lee.

"I don't – but I'm still scared of them!" Jaz grinned.

"So this is just a bit of fun – right?" said Mo. "Got a wine glass?"

"In the kitchen," I said. "OK, I'll get it."

When I came back, someone had turned off most of the lights. There was just the lamp in the corner. Mo took the glass and turned it upside down in the middle of the table.

"Now what?" said Lee.

"Now we all sit round the table," she said. "We each put one finger on top of the glass. And we wait."

Chapter Three

Is There Anybody There?

It was kind of spooky, sitting there in the half-light. Waiting for something to happen. I kept telling myself it was OK. There are no ghosts, right?

It was still pretty spooky.

"Maybe I will have that pizza," said Lee.

"Sit down, Lee!" said Mo.

He sat down.

"Put your finger back on the glass," she said. With Mo, it's always easier to do what she says.

The moment Lee touched the glass again, it began to slide around the table.

Mo said, "Is there anybody there?"

The glass shot across the table and stopped at NO.

Jaz giggled.

"Oh, very funny, Mo," said Lee. "You almost had us going there."

"It wasn't me," she said. "It was all of us together. It takes more than one person to make the glass move."

"Says who?" I said.

"Says anyone who's ever tried it," snapped Mo. Like she was some sort of expert. "We all agreed we don't believe in ghosts. Right?" she said. "So when I said, 'Is there anybody there?' the answer we got was NO." She looked round at us all and smiled. "But what if we decided the answer was going to be YES? Shall we give it a try? Just for a laugh."

I shrugged. "Why not?"

"I'm up for it," said Lee.

Jaz wasn't happy, but she nodded. "OK."

"Let's make it more interesting," said Mo. "Let's give our ghost a name."

She turned to me. "Scott, what do you think we should call it?"

"Me?" I asked.

"Just think of a name," she snapped.

"OK... Let's call him Tom," I said.

"Jaz!" said Mo. "Think of a number, between 16 and 40. We don't want our ghost to be some little kid or some horrible old man."

"21, then," said Jaz.

"So our ghost is called Tom," said Mo, "and he was 21 when he died. Let's make it not too long ago. How about World War Two?"

We'd been doing World War Two in history.

"A bomber pilot!" Lee said suddenly. "The plane's coming back from a raid over Germany. There's an engine on fire. The crew have bailed out, but the pilot has to stay at the controls so the plane doesn't crash on the town. He saves the town, but he goes down in flames."

Next to rubbish horror films, Lee loves war movies.

"OK," said Mo. "Got that, everyone? Right! Fingers on the glass. And think of Tom."

I stared hard at my finger resting on the glass. The glass didn't move. It wasn't going to.

"Think of Tom!" Mo said again.

I was wishing I'd just settled for a night in on my own when I heard Jaz catch her breath. The glass was on the move again.

"Don't let go!" cried Mo. "Think of Tom! Is there anybody there?"

The glass slid sideways and stopped at the card marked YES.

"Yes!" shouted Lee. "Result!"

"Shut up," said Mo. She asked the glass, "Who are you?"

The glass slid off again.

It went to the U. Then to NO.

"U NO." I laughed. "You know! Of course we know."

"Look," cried Mo. "He's texting!"

"**We** are texting, Mo," I said. "We made him up. Remember?"

Mo gave me a nasty look. "Tom," she said, "can you spell your name for us?"

The glass picked out T, then O, then M, faster than any of us could spot where the letters were, because they weren't in any sort of order.

"This is scary," said Jaz. "I don't like it."

"Next question," said Mo, ignoring her. "Tom, when did you die?"

The glass spelled out the letters:

NOT DEAD

"He doesn't know he's dead," said Mo. "I think you often get that with ghosts."

"He's not dead," I said, "because he was never alive."

The glass was on the move again.

U R

"You are! He's texting again!" cried Mo.

U R

SO

WRONG

Mo grinned.

"He's talking to you, Scott," she said. "He's telling you, you are so wrong."

"I don't like this," said Jaz. "Let's stop."

"We can't stop now," said Mo. "Tom, why are you here? What do you want?"

The glass spelled out:

TO LIVE

"To live!" said Mo. "He wants to live."

The glass began sliding all over the table, faster and faster. Jaz cried out, "I'm not doing this any more!"

As soon as her finger left the glass, it spun off the table, flew through the air and smashed on the floor.

"Wow!" said Lee.

Jaz was crying. Mo put an arm round her.

"I'll take you home," she said.

She gave Lee and me a nasty look, like this whole stupid game had been our idea, not hers.

***

After the girls had gone, I cleared up the broken glass. Then Lee and me had that pizza. I didn't bother with the oven, just bunged it in the microwave. Not a good idea.

Then Lee went off on his bike. I watched him ride away, into the dark.

Chapter Four

Accident?

I knew if I went to bed I wouldn't sleep. So I sat up waiting for Mum.

She was late. It's like that in A and E, weekends and holidays. There's always a rush late evening and there's never enough staff.

Several times I thought I heard her moving about the house. I thought she must have come in and I hadn't noticed. But there was no car on the drive.

Once, I found the front door wide open.

I shut it and went round every room in the house, checking all the doors and windows.

I still had a feeling I wasn't alone.

When Mum came in she found me watching TV, but I had one eye on the window and the other on the door.

The first thing she said was, "Why aren't you in bed?"

"I wasn't sleepy," I said.

"Why have you got all the lights on?"

"Are they?" I said. "Sorry."

I wasn't going to tell her I'd been scared. Scared to turn the lights off. Scared of going to bed alone in an empty house.

"You're late," I said.

Then it was her turn to say sorry. "I was just getting my coat on," she said, "when they brought in a boy who'd been knocked off his bike by a car. As soon as I saw who it was, I knew I had to stay."

"Who was it?" I asked.

"It was your friend Lee. The driver said he swerved right out in front of him. There was nothing he could do."

I said, "Is he dead?"

"Dead?" she said. "No, of course not. But he was lucky the car wasn't going any faster. And why wasn't he wearing a helmet? As it is, he's got a broken nose and a broken arm. But he was awake and talking to us. He was going on and on about someone called Tom."

"Tom?" I said.

"He said he'd seen him," said Mum. "He said the accident was Tom's fault, for stepping out in front of him. He told me to tell you to take care."

She looked worried. "This Tom – is he someone from school? Has he been bullying you? You would tell me, wouldn't you?"

"Of course I would, Mum." (Not!) "Don't worry," I said. "I can handle it."

***

I went round to Jaz's as soon as Mum let me out of the house next morning. Mo was already there.

"I hope you're pleased with yourself, Mo," I said. "You and your pal, whoever he is. Lee could have been killed last night!"

"What are you talking about?" said Mo.

"Don't pretend you don't know!" I said. "You set this up! And we fell for it. And now Lee's in hospital."

"Lee's in hospital?" said Jaz.

I told her about the accident. And what Lee said, about Tom stepping out in front of him.

"Lee saw him? That is just so spooky!" said Mo.

"Like you didn't plan it!" I said. "Who was it? Some mate of yours, kitted up like a World War Two bomber pilot? Bet you had a good laugh when you saw the ambulance carting Lee away!"

"Shut up a minute!" yelled Mo. "Take a look at this."

I grabbed the bit of paper she was waving. It was a picture of a man in a flying jacket.

"Jaz drew it," said Mo. "This morning. Before I even got here," she added.

I looked at Jaz. They'd had plenty of time to cook up a story between them. But Jaz isn't like that.

I said, "You drew this before Mo got here?"

Jaz nodded. I believed her.

"She's seen him too, Scott," said Mo.

Jaz draws pictures of people. It's what she does, all the time, in lessons or watching TV or waiting for a bus, whenever. And she's good. I mean, really good.

"I had this dream," Jaz said. "When I woke up, I drew that picture. I kind of knew it was him."

"You mean Tom?" I said.

Jaz nodded again.

Mo folded up the picture and put it in her pocket. "We won't say anything," she said. "We'll show the picture to Lee and see what he says, OK?"

Chapter Five

Pictures of Tom

Lee was still in the hospital but they were going to let him out later that day.

The nurse said they'd given him a brain scan and found nothing there.

"I mean, nothing to worry about," she said, after we all fell about laughing.

He still looked pretty bad. The broken nose had come with a side order of two black eyes. I'd have taken one look in the mirror and stuck a bag over my head. But I'm not Lee.

"You should have seen me, guys!" he crowed. "It was just like in the movies. I went head first over the handlebars – rolled over the bonnet of the car – then splat! I'm flat on my back and he's vanished into thin air!"

"You mean Tom?" I said.

"I saw him! Did your mum tell you? I saw our ghost!"

"You don't believe in ghosts," I said.

"I do now! I've got to, haven't I?" he said.

Mo chipped in. "Take a look at this." She showed him the picture Jaz had drawn.

"That's him!" said Lee. He looked from Mo, to Jaz, to me, then back again at Mo. "Where did you get it?" he said.

"Jaz drew it," I said.

"She's seen him too," said Mo.

"Only in my dreams," said Jaz.

"You're kidding!" said Lee. "In your dreams? That is just so – wow!"

"Are you sure it's him?" I said. "This is the guy that made you swerve in front of the car?"

"Sure I'm sure. He stepped right out in front of me," said Lee.

"How did you know it was Tom?" I asked.

He thought about it. "The flying jacket. The boots. He wasn't old, but his hair was cut like my grandad's. And he had this dinky little moustache." Lee ran a finger across, like he was drawing a pencil line under his nose. "He just looked like he'd stepped out of some old war movie."

"And what made you think he was a ghost?" I asked him.

"The road was empty," said Lee. "Then he was there, in front of me. Next minute he was gone. **And** the driver of the car didn't see him."

I said, "Maybe he was too busy watching you going head over heels."

"Scott thinks I set the whole thing up," said Mo.

"No way!" said Lee.

I still didn't buy it.

As we were coming away, Jaz said to me, "I saw him, too! In my dreams. What have we done?"

I said, "We fooled around with a stupid pack of cards. You had a bad dream. That's all."

"What about Lee?" she said. "He recognised Tom from my picture."

I said, "You know Lee. He spends half his life watching horror movies. Someone steps out in front of him. Next day Mo shows him a picture. And he kids himself he saw a ghost."

"And that's all you think happened?"

"That's all," I said.

***

Three days later my phone rang.

"Scott?" It was Jaz.

"What is it?" I said. "What's wrong?"

"Can you come round?" she asked.

"Give me ten minutes," I said.

I was there in five. That's how worried she sounded.

She'd been drawing more pictures. The walls of her room were covered in them. The rest were on the bed and over the floor.

They were all pictures of the same man she'd drawn after that first evening. The man the others said had to be Tom.

"I can't get him out of my head, Scott," she said. "I close my eyes and he's there, even before I fall asleep. When I sleep, I get these dreams."

"Good dreams? Bad dreams?" I asked.

Jaz shook her head. "I don't know!" she said. "I can never remember. All I know is, when I wake up, I have to start drawing again."

I said, "Have you told Mo?"

Mo started this. It was all down to Mo.

"I've texted her," said Jaz. "Left messages. She's not answering."

Chapter Six

Shadows

I looked for Mo in all the usual places. The shopping mall. The music shop and the cafes. I even tried her house.

Her mum said she thought she'd gone to the library.

The library? Mo? Still, I'd looked everywhere else, so I headed for the library. A short cut took me through the skate park.

Lee had the place to himself that day. Maybe one look at him had scared the others off. He looked like something left over from Halloween.

One broken nose, two black eyes and an arm in plaster, and he was still pulling kickflips and fakies. All the time I was talking to him, he never stopped.

"Seen Mo?" I said.

"Maybe," said Lee, sliding past me. "Is it about the other night?" he asked.

"No," I said. "Maybe. Why?"

"You still think she set it up," he said as he slid back the other way.

"Don't **you**?" I said.

"I don't see how she could have done," he said. "Bomber pilot was my idea. So how did this mate of hers get hold of the right outfit in time?"

"Maybe she texted him while we weren't looking."

"I could have said a fireman, or an ambulance driver," Lee said.

"Come on, Lee! Mo knows you love war movies."

Backwards and forwards he slid. Up to the top of the ramp, then down again. I was starting to feel seasick just watching.

"He'd have needed a whole rack of clothes standing by," said Lee. "I know what I saw. I saw a ghost."

"How can you have seen him? We made him up!" I said.

"Maybe we picked up on something that really happened. Mo thinks that's our best bet. She's in the library now, checking it out."

"Mo's in the library?" I asked. "Cheers! That's all I wanted to know."

I found her in the basement. That's where they keep the old local papers on microfilm. Mo was scrolling through them, page by page.

"Any luck?" I said.

She shook her head, scowling. "This thing is, like, out of the Stone Age! No index – no nothing. It's doing my head in!"

She switched off the machine and pushed back her chair.

"I'm just going to have to fake it," she said. "After all, who's going to check?"

"Check what? Fake what?" I said.

"The story," she said. "About Tom? The bomber pilot who gave his life to save the town? For my history project?"

"You're going to make this your history project?" I said. "I thought we were supposed to be doing Life on the Home Front?"

"What – write about ration books and air-raid shelters? Boring!" she said. "What about the true story of the bomber plane that almost wiped out half the town? That's totally Life on the Home Front!"

"Not if it didn't happen," I said.

"It could have done. I'll say I've been talking to the old people," she said. "I'll say I met this old lady. She had this friend who was in love with a bomber pilot. The friend worked in the RAF control room, but she wasn't on duty the night the pilot died."

"So?" I said.

"So the pilot never got to say goodbye. That's why his ghost can't rest. Is that worth an A star, or what?"

"No, because you just made it up," I said.

"Tom wants to live!" she said. "So I'm giving him a life. The place where Lee saw him was just open fields in those days. That could be the place where the plane came down."

I gave it one last shot. "But it **never happened**. Tom's not real! We made him up. Remember?"

Mo didn't answer. She just got up and walked out of the library.

I followed her out onto the street. It was past four in the afternoon, and already dark.

I realised I'd forgotten to tell her about Jaz. The pictures. The dreams.

I called after her, "Mo! Wait! You've got to talk to Jaz!"

I think she heard me. But she didn't look back.

I watched her walk away, her shadow changing shape as she moved from one street lamp to the next.

The odd thing was, she seemed to have not one shadow, but two. Like there was somebody walking beside her, but all I could see was his shadow.

I told myself it was a trick of the light.

Then one of the shadows stopped.

Mo walked on, along with her own shadow. The other shadow stood very still. Slowly it turned its head towards me. I felt it looking at me, checking me out.

Then it began to move.

I didn't wait to see any more. I ran.

***

Safe in my room, I tried to get my head round what just happened. What was it I saw?

A shadow? Yes.

No!

That thing I saw was more than a shadow. That thing had a mind of its own.

A ghost, then? What ghost? The ghost of Tom, the bomber pilot?

How could it be? We made him up.

But maybe that's what ghosts are. If enough people believe hard enough – there's your ghost. It could be a mad monk, or a black dog, or a queen with her head tucked under her arm.

Together we'd created our very own ghost. He had nearly killed Lee. Now he was haunting Jaz and stalking Mo.

What about me?

I'd got away this time. Maybe all I had to do now was stay away from shadows. But on Monday I'd be back at school, walking home in the dark. Walking home in a world full of shadows.

Chapter Seven

Bonfire Night

I didn't see the others again till Bonfire Night. Bonfire Night on the estate is always on Friday so as not to clash with the big fireworks show in town on the Saturday.

There's a patch of waste ground down the end where they were going to build more houses. Then they didn't. So that's where we have the bonfire and the fireworks. There's live music and dancing too. And hamburgers and hot dogs and baked potatoes and candyfloss. A beer tent for the adults and a roundabout for the little kids.

It's good. I mean, really good.

I went round with Lee in the morning, collecting stuff for the bonfire. I had to push the cart because of Lee's arm being in plaster but I didn't mind. It was great seeing the bonfire pile up – and up – and up. We were going to make this one the biggest ever.

It was dark by the time we finished. All the helpers got a free Coke. As we were leaving, Lee said, "Have you seen the guy?"

Every year there's a competition for the best guy. The winning guy gets to be burnt on the bonfire, which I think is a pretty rubbish prize.

"Come on," said Lee. "Come and look!" So I came and I looked.

"It's him, isn't it?" I said.

The guy was wearing a flying jacket and helmet. It even had a little moustache pencilled on the face.

I said, "Was this your idea?"

"A bit," said Lee. "My little brother and his mates did all the work. What do you think?"

"I think it looks evil," I said.

There was something about the black button eyes. The lipstick smile.

I said, "Just don't let Mo see it."

"You don't think she'll like it?" asked Lee.

"Trust me," I said. "She won't."

"Wanna bet?" said Lee. "Hey, girls! Take a look at this."

They came. They looked. "What is **that**?" said Mo.

"I told you she wouldn't like it," I muttered. "Let's get out of here."

Lee didn't hear me. He crouched down beside the guy, lifted one of its arms, and flapped it up and down.

"Say hello to your boyfriend, Mo! Say hello to Tom! 'Hello, Mo!'" he said in a squeaky voice.

"My boyfriend?" Mo swung round. "What have you been telling him, Jaz?" she demanded.

Jaz shook her head. "Nothing. I swear!"

Mo turned back to Lee. "That thing is supposed to be Tom?" she said.

"I think it looks evil," I said.

Mo took another long, hard look.

"I don't," she said. "I think he looks cute." Lee nudged me. "What did I say?" he muttered. "She fancies him."

When I looked back at Mo, she had her eyes fixed on the guy like the rest of us weren't even there.

"Come on, Jaz," I said. "I'll buy you a hot dog."

While we were waiting in the queue, I said, "Did you talk to Mo? About the pictures?"

Jaz nodded. "We're working together on the project now. It's going to be like a graphic novel. She's doing the story. I'm doing the pictures."

"You're OK with that?" I asked.

"I'm OK," said Jaz. "It's like all the stuff I was dreaming about was all mixed up. Mo's helped me sort it out."

Why was Mo mad at you when Lee said Tom was her boyfriend?"

Jaz shook her head and bit into her hot dog. "I think Mo is a bit in love with Tom. But I didn't tell Lee!"

"And you're sure you're OK?"

"I'm OK," she said. "I told you."

I saw they'd placed the guy on top of the bonfire. Flames were already licking at it. Mo was standing where we'd left her, close to the bonfire, looking up at the guy. There was an odd look on her face. Like the look girls get when their favourite pop star is on the TV.

Then it happened.

You know that game where you take it in turns to build a tower until someone puts a bit on wrong and the whole lot comes tumbling down?

That's what was happening to the bonfire now.

I saw the guy begin to topple.

I saw Mo standing there, looking up, as the burning guy tumbled towards her with its arms outspread.

"Mo!" I yelled. "Get out of the way!"

She didn't move. Maybe there was too much noise. Maybe she just didn't hear.

I threw away my hot dog and started running.

Out of the corner of my eye I saw the guy slowly falling.

I felt the heat of the flames on my cheek.

I crashed into Mo so hard we landed several yards away.

Mo pushed me off. "Why did you do that?" she snarled. Then she saw the guy on fire in the place where she'd been standing.

"Oh no," she said.

"Didn't you see it, Mo?" I asked her. "Why didn't you move?"

Mo shook her head. "I don't know. He was looking at me and I was looking at him leaning towards me. Then – wham! – bam! That was you, thumping into me."

The bonfire was scattered all over the place. People were shouting and running and putting out small fires. Mo went over to where the guy lay with little flames licking round its face and hands. She gave it a good, hard kick.

"You are so dead!" she said. "Dead! Dead! Dead!" Each time she said it, she gave the guy another kick.

The guy just lay there, slowly burning, and smiling that evil smile.

Chapter Eight

Nobody There

All four of us met at Jaz's house the next morning.

The walls were still covered in pictures, but now they were telling a story.

There wasn't much about the plane crash. This was more of a love story. The girl looked like Mo.

"I can't draw people out of my head," said Jaz. "I have to have a real person to copy."

"What about Tom?" I said.

"Tom was different. That's what scared me."

"He's evil," I said. I told them about the shadow that chased me home from the library. "You saw what happened last night, with the guy and the bonfire. We have to get rid of him, before one of us gets hurt."

"How do we do that?" said Lee.

"I've got an idea," I said.

I'd been thinking about it all night long. I still wasn't sure if it would work.

I said, "Before it all started, we all agreed we didn't believe in ghosts. So when Mo said, 'Is there anybody there?' the answer we got was no. Right? Then we made up a ghost. Suddenly, he's there. I was the last one to see him. I think that's because I was the last one to believe in him."

"I think I see," Lee said slowly.

Jaz said, "You mean all we have to do is stop believing – and he'll go away?"

"It's worth a try," said Mo. "Maybe if we did it in the same place, with the cards and everything."

"No problem," I said. "My mum's on duty again this evening. We'll have the house to ourselves."

Mo began pulling the pictures off the walls. "We can start by getting rid of these," she said.

"What shall we do with them?" said Jaz. "Burn them?"

"We'll shred them," said Mo. "My dad's got a shredder."

I said, "What about your history project, Mo?"

"What do you think?" she said. "After last night? I've deleted it."

"There goes your A star," I said.

"I was never going to get an A star."

"So what are you going to do now?" I asked.

Mo shrugged. "Pull something off the internet, I suppose. Same as usual."

I said, "You've still got all day Sunday. My gran lent me three shoe boxes of stuff about the Home Front. There's masses of it I'm not going to use. Come round if you like."

"I might," she said. "Thanks, anyway."

Mo's not so bad when you get to know her.

***

So, anyway, there we sat in my house that Saturday evening, just as we'd sat on Halloween. We'd turned out the lights, except for the lamp in the corner. Mo had laid out the cards in a circle on the table.

Jaz whispered to me, "Do you think he knows what we're doing?"

I said, "Who are you talking about?" Jaz bit her lip. "Sorry," she said. "No-one."

"We're just having a bit of fun," said Mo. "Like we did the other evening. Nothing's going to happen."

"Who believes in ghosts? Not me!" said Lee.

"Ghosts?" I said. "Not in this house."

Jaz shivered. "I'm cold," she said.

"Let's get started," said Mo. "Fingers on the glass, everyone."

So we sat, each with one finger resting on the glass until the glass began to move. "Do we believe in ghosts?" said Mo.

As soon as it started heading for the YES card, Lee stood up. "Any Coke in the fridge, Scott?"

"Help yourself," I said.

Lee went to the kitchen, came back with a can, and we all settled down again.

That's how we played it. Mo kept asking the same question. "Do we believe in ghosts?" Every time we looked like getting the answer YES, one of us would chip in.

I thought Tom would fight back. I thought it would be like you see in the movies. Things flying through the air. Mirrors shattering. One of us talking in a funny voice. Maybe even a small fire.

Instead – nothing.

Maybe that's why, in the end, we really did give up believing.

"Do we believe in ghosts?" said Mo.

The glass slid to NO. And stayed there.

After a bit, Jaz said, "I can smell burning." But it was only because I'd put the oven on to warm up.

"Anyone for pizza?" I said.

Chapter Nine

All the Time

On Sunday I got out all the stuff Gran had lent me for my history project. There were three shoe boxes full. I put the one with the photos in on one side.

The others were full of all sorts of stuff.

There were ration books and pages of old newspapers, and Gran's ID from the day she was born, and a letter from the King to her dad to thank him for being in the Home Guard.

The cookery books were what I was after. And the handy hints her mum had cut out of the papers and magazines. I was going to do Food in Wartime.

Something fell out. I picked it up.

It was a photo of a man in a flying jacket. He had this really old-fashioned haircut and a dinky little moustache. I knew who it was before I turned it over and saw what was written on the back.

Tom. July 1943.

"Ghosts?" I'd said. "Not in this house."

But he'd been here all the time.

So why don't I destroy it? Burn it. Shred it. Chuck it in the bin. Then there'd be nothing left.

I just can't do it.

"What do you want?" Mo had asked him. And he said: TO LIVE.

That's not much to ask.

I don't think he meant Lee to get knocked off his bike by a car. I don't think he meant to frighten Jaz by creeping into her dreams.

Mo was trying to give him what he wanted.

She was giving him a life, even if it was made up. She got Jaz to draw her over and over again as his girlfriend. Maybe in the end he thought she **was** his girlfriend. When he brought the bonfire tumbling down I don't think he meant to hurt her. Maybe he just wanted to say goodbye.

I was the one who said he was evil. I was the one who said we had to get rid of him. That's why I'm scared now.

Scared of the footsteps on the landing. Scared of the shadow creeping under my bedroom door. Scared of being alone.

Scared that I'm not alone.

Bonus Bits!

Guess Who

Each piece of information below is about one of the characters in the story. Can you match them up? Check your answers at the end of this section.

A Named the ghost Tom.

B Draws lots of pictures of the ghost

C Stays at the hospital when she hears about Lee

D Brought 'Planet of the Undead' DVD to watch

E Started working with Jaz to write a graphic novel

1. Mo

2. Lee

3. Mum

4. Scott

5. Jaz

Historical Facts

Bomber crews in World War II were made up of men from UK and other countries, e.g. Poland, France, Norway and more.

Most aircrew were aged between 19 and 25, although some were even as young as 16 years old. It is also known that at least one was in his sixties!

Out of about 125,000 aircrew in World War II, nearly half were killed and many more were wounded. It was a very dangerous job.

Using a Narrator

In this story, Scott is the narrator so is writing in the first person (using I). This is different to lots of other stories as it means that we are seeing the events from Scott's point of view. We find out what he is experiencing as well as what he is thinking about the events that are unfolding. We also find out what he thinks about his friends and their actions. Can you think of any other stories you have read that have a character as a narrator?

What Next?

Have a think about these questions after reading this story.

- Do you think Scott and his friends were sensible to play the game they did when Scott's mum was at work? Why/why not?

- How do you think Scott feels now and do you think he is happy? Why/why not?

ANSWERS to GUESS WHO

1E, 2D, 3C, 4A, 5B

Also available from Bloomsbury Education

Nic can't risk giving his friends another excuse to laugh at him, so when the boys visit the local haunted house after a party he accepts a dare to go inside.

The trouble is, the boys don't realise that this party has a host, and he isn't very friendly...

For more great books visit www.bloomsbury.com

978-1-4729-6083-2   978-1-4729-4411-5   978-1-4729-3487-1

978-1-4729-4428-3   978-1-4729-1181-0   978-1-4729-1066-0